W9-AWD-387

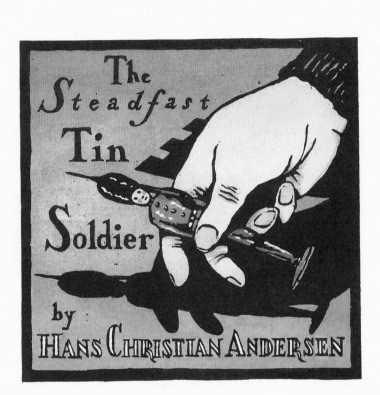

A DK PUBLISHING BOOK

First American Edition, 1996
2 4 6 8 10 9 7 5 3 1

Published in the United States by DK Publishing, Inc.
95 Madison Avenue,
New York, New York 10016

Copyright © 1996 Dorling Kindersley Limited, London
Text copyright © 1996 Adrian Mitchell
Illustrations copyright © 1996 Jonathan Heale

The author's and illustrator's moral rights have been asserted.

All rights reserved under International and Pan-American Copyright Conventions. No
part of this publication may be reproduced, stored in a retrieval system, or transmit-
ted in any form or by any means, electronic, mechanical, photocopying, recording, or
otherwise, without the prior written permission of the copyright owner.
Published in Great Britain by Dorling Kindersley Limited.

Distributed by Houghton Mifflin Company, Boston.

A CIP catalog record is available from the Library of Congress.

ISBN 1-56458-310-4

Color reproduction by Dot Gradations Ltd.
Printed in Hong Kong by Wing King Tong

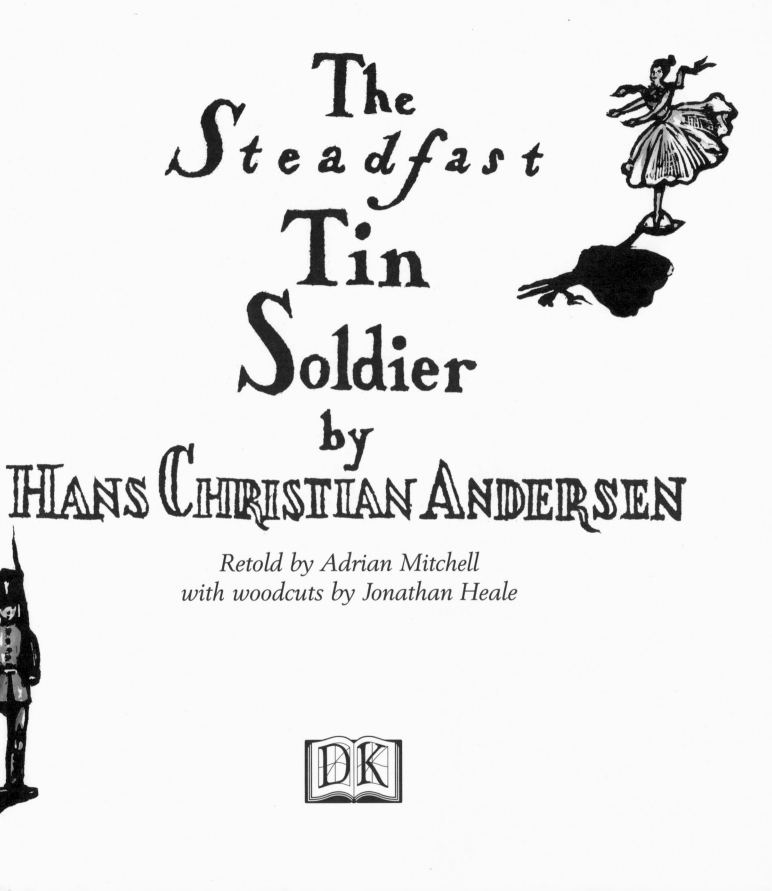

The Steadfast Tin Soldier

by
Hans Christian Andersen

Retold by Adrian Mitchell
with woodcuts by Jonathan Heale

Five times five is twenty-five,
And there were once twenty-five tin soldiers.
They were all brothers, for they'd all been made
Out of the same old melted-down tin spoon.

Muskets on their shoulders,
Stiffly at attention,
Smart as paint
In their red and blue uniforms.

Twenty-five tin soldiers
Lying in their box.
When the lid was opened,
The first words they heard were
"Tin soldiers!"
From a happy little,
Huge little boy,
Clapping his hands on his birthday.

Twenty-five tin soldiers.
He stood them on a table
In five lines of five.
Every soldier was like all the other soldiers
Except for one. He was just a little different.

He was the last to be made,
When there was only a small blob of tin left –
Not quite enough for a whole tin soldier.
So he only had one leg.
But he stood as steadfast on his one tin leg
As his brothers stood upon two.
And of all the twenty-five tin soldiers
He was the only one
Who became an astonishing person.

The one-legged soldier
Looked down the birthday table
With all its higgledy-piggledy presents.
He gazed toward the uttermost end of the table,
And there stood a wonderful castle of cardboard,
With pipe-cleaner trees and a looking-glass lake.

And there were wax swans swimming on the lake,
Watching their reflections jealously.
All this was very lovely,
But loveliest of all
Was the miniature lady
In the castle's open doorway.

She was made out of paper.
Her dress was lightest muslin.
Around her shoulders
She wore a blue ribbon,
And in the middle of the ribbon
Shone a rose made of tinsel.
And the rose was the same size
As her lovely oval face.

She was a ballet dancer, so she stood
With her arms stretching out
As if to welcome someone to a hug.
She was a ballet dancer, so she stood
On the tips of the toes of one leg.
The other leg was folded up
And hidden in her skirt.
So the tin soldier believed
She only had one leg, the same as him.

"She'd make the right wife for me,"
He thought, "but she's so posh.
And she lives in a wonderful castle.
All I've got to live in is a box –
And there's twenty-five of us billeted in there.
You couldn't ask a lady to move in.
All the same, I wish I could meet her."

He carefully hid himself away
Behind a toy lamppost.
And from there he watched the little dancer.
And she continued to stand on one leg,
Never ever losing her balance.

On the evening of that birthday
The huge little boy was put to bed,
And twenty-four tin soldiers
Were placed on their backs in their box.

All the other toys began to play.
The jump rope lassoed the rocking horse.
The marbles tobogganed down the inky desk-lid.
The Noah's Ark animals played Hopcrocodile,
Climb the Greasy Giraffe, and Blind-Bear's-Buff.

The twenty-four tin soldiers
Rattled in their box,
For they wanted to join in,
But their lid had been carefully clicked shut.
There was such a racket that the parrot woke up
And told them all off, in rhyming verse.

There were only two who did not move at all –
The one-legged soldier and the dancer.
She stood on the tips of the toes of one leg,
Never ever losing her balance.
Nor did the one-legged soldier lose his balance.
They both stood fast,
And his eyes were watching her eyes all the time.

The clock struck midnight.
Bloompk!
The Jack-in-the-Box jumped out of his box
And laughed in the face of the one-legged soldier.
"Tin soldier," said the Jack,
"She's not for you."
But the tin soldier pretended not to hear.

On his after-birthday morning
The huge little boy got out of bed
And he put the tin soldier
On the windowsill.
Now it may have been that Jack-in-the-Box,
It may have been a draft,
But whatever it was
The window flew open
And down fell the soldier,
Head over heels,
From the third-floor window,
Past the second-floor window,
And the first-floor window,
To the street below,
Into a gaping canyon
Between two paving stones.
His bayonet stuck
Into gray clay
And his one leg pointed at the Sun.

The boy ran out
And nearly stepped on him,
But couldn't find him anywhere.
If the soldier had called out
"Help! I'm here!"
The boy might have found him.
But the soldier thought that to shout like that
Would not be very soldierly.

It began to rain –
One drop, then two,
Then twenty-four, then thousands.
When the rain stopped,
Two raggedy boys strolled by.
"Hang on," said one, "there's a tin soldier.
Let's give him a trip on a boat."

So he folded a stray newspaper
Into a boat,
And he stood the soldier in it
And launched him down the gutter.
The raggedy boys ran along beside him,
Cheering him on.

The waves were wild
And the current was cruel,
For the gutter was at full flood.
The newspaper boat pitched and tossed
And sometimes whirled around and around so fast
The tin soldier trembled.
But he stayed at his post,
Steadfast as ever,
Musket on his shoulder,
Staring straight ahead.

Suddenly the boat shot under
A stone bridge curving over the gutter
And the soldier was in darkness,
Darkness that seemed to get darker and darker.
"Where am I going?" the tin soldier wondered.
"This is the work of that Jack-in-the-Box!
If only the dancing lady was here –
It could be twice as dark, but I wouldn't care."

An enormous rat, who lived down the gutter,
Held out a slimy paw and cried,
"Where's your passport?
Where's your permit?"
But the soldier said nothing
And held his musket tighter,
Steadfastly.

The boat flew past, the rat flew after it.
He gnashed his daggery teeth and squealed,
"Stop him! No passport! No permit!
Customs and Immigration! Stop that soldier!"

But the river flowed even more furiously
And the tin soldier could just see
A half-lemon shape of light where the tunnel ended.
But at the same time he could hear
The mighty rushing sound of water,
A thunder to terrify the bravest of the brave.

For where the bridge ended,
The waters widened
Into a great falling sheet descending
Into the steaming mouth of a sewer.
Imagine you're sitting in a canoe
Five feet from the edge of Niagara Falls …

The boat sped on.
The tin soldier stood
Still and straight,
Unblinking, steadfast.

The boat spun around
And around and around
Till it filled with water
Up to the brim
And sinking fast,
And the tin soldier, standing,
Up to his neck
In the wild water
And sinking faster,
Deeper and deeper,
And the waterlogged boat,
Soggy and shredding,
And the waters closing
Over the tin head
Of the tin soldier.

He thought about the dancer,
Who he'd never see again.
Inside his ears he could just hear
Somebody singing an old song –
"Onward, Soldier! You'll have the satisfaction
Of an honorable death in action!"
And then the newspaper boat fell all to pieces
And the tin soldier tumbled downward and downward
To be swallowed by a gigantic fish.

Oh! It was dark inside that fish!
It was worse than the fall from the windowsill.
It was worse than the rapids in the gutter.
It was worse than the rat with the slimy paw.
It was narrow and terrible in that fish's gullet.
But the tin soldier was still brave,
And he lay in that fish with his musket on his shoulder.

The fish swam and swam, twisting and leaping
Like a contortionist on hot bricks.
And then that great fish was still.
There was a flash of lightning.
There was daylight.
A voice called out,
"Look! It's that tin soldier!"

The fish had been caught,
Taken to market,
Sold, and brought back to a kitchen
Where the cook opened it up with a knife.
She picked up the soldier by the waist,
Held him between her finger and thumb,
And carried him into the living room
Where everyone clapped their hands when they saw
The famous tin soldier
Who had traveled the world inside a fish.

But the soldier wasn't proud.
He was placed on the table and then he saw –
Incredible things happen all the time! –
He saw he was back in the birthday room.
He saw the same huge little boy,
And the same toys on the same table,
And the same castle and the same dancer.
She was still standing
On the tips of the toes of one leg
With the other leg folded up –
Yes, she was steadfast, too.

The tin soldier was so moved
That he almost wept tin tears –
But he stopped himself.
That would have been unsoldierly.
He looked at her
And she looked at him,
But he said nothing
And she said not a word.

Suddenly the boy grabbed hold of the soldier
And flung him, headfirst, into the red-hot fire.
He couldn't say why –
He didn't know why …
Maybe the Jack-in-the-Box knew –
But nobody asked him.

Now the tin soldier
Was illuminated by the flames.
He felt as hot as the inside of the Sun,
But he didn't know
If the heat came from the fire
Or from his love.
The red and blue of his uniform were gone,
But nobody knew if they were worn away
By sorrow or hard traveling.

He looked at his dancer
And she looked at him –
And he felt himself melting away.
But still he stood firm
With his musket on his shoulder.

Somebody opened the birthday-room door –
The draft caught up the dancer
And she flew like a paper fairy
Into the fire,
Beside the tin soldier.

And she was gone in the flames
At the very same moment
That the tin soldier melted.